C000155740

The *Supernatural* Quiz Book Season 3

500 questions and answers on
Supernatural Season 3

By Light Bulb Quizzes
Written by fans, for fans

Unofficial

Published by Light Bulb Quizzes

First edition (July 2015)

©Light Bulb Quizzes 2015

All rights reserved.
Subject to statutory exception and to provisions of
relevant collective licensing agreements, no part of this
publication may be reproduced without the prior written
permission of the author(s).

The moral right of Light Bulb Quizzes
to be identified as the author(s)
of this book has been asserted in accordance with
the Copyright, Designs and Patents Act 1988

ISBN 978-0993203022

Edited by

Kim Kimber

www.kimkimber.co.uk

Cover image by

Devin Davis-Lorton

www.devinternet.tumblr.com

All of the questions in this quiz book are based on the DVD release of *Supernatural* Season 3, produced by Warner Home Video and the soundtrack and other details may sometimes vary from that of other versions.

This book is unofficial and unauthorised. All of the questions have been researched and compiled by Light Bulb Quizzes who have done their best to ensure that all information is correct. However, if any sharp-eyed *Supernatural* fans notice an error, please contact us so that it can be rectified.

For all fans of
Supernatural

CONTENTS

Introduction 1

Questions 3

Episode 1 – The Magnificent Seven 5

Episode 2 – The Kids are Alright...................................7

Jensen Ackles (Dean Winchester)...................................9

Jared Padalecki (Sam Winchester)................................10

Episode 3 – Bad Day at Black Rock 11

Episode 4 – Sin City 13

Episode Titles..14

Name the Episode..15

Episode 5 – Bedtime Stories 17

Episode 6 – Red Sky at Morning 19

Supernatural Quotes..20

Cast Appearances...21

Episode 7 – Fresh Blood 23

Episode 8 – A Very Supernatural Christmas 24

Katie Cassidy (Ruby) 26

Lauren Cohen (Bela Talbot) 27

Episode 9 – Malleus Maleficarum 28

Episode 10 – Dream a Little Dream of Me 30

Supernatural Soundtrack...32

Monsters and Demons...33

Episode 11 – Mystery Spot...34

Episode 12 – Jus in Bello 36

Cindy Sampson (Lisa Braeden) 38

Nicholas Elia (Ben Braeden) 39

Episode 13 – Ghostfacers...40

Episode 14 – Long-Distance Call 42

Sterling K. Brown (Gordon Walker)...............................44

Richard Speight Jr (Trickster) 45

Episode 15 – Time is on My Side 46

Episode 16 – No Rest for the Wicked 48

Production, Crew and Writing 49

Supernatural Trivia 50

Answers 53

Episode 1 – The Magnificent Seven...............................55

Episode 2 – The Kids are Alright...................................57

Jensen Ackles (Dean Winchester)..................................59

Jared Padalecki (Sam Winchester)................................60

Episode 3 – Bad Day at Black Rock 61

Episode 4 – Sin City 63

Episode Titles..64

Name the Episode..65

Episode 5 – Bedtime Stories.....................................66

Episode 6 – Red Sky at Morning.................................67

Supernatural Quotes...68

Cast Appearances..69

Episode 7 – Fresh Blood...70

Episode 8 – A Very Supernatural Christmas.......................71

Katie Cassidy (Ruby)..73

Lauren Cohen (Bela Talbot)......................................74

Episode 9 – Malleus Maleficarum................................75

Episode 10 – Dream a Little Dream of Me........................76

Supernatural Soundtrack.......................................77

Monsters and Demons...78

Episode 11 – Mystery Spot.......................................79

Episode 12 – Jus in Bello......................................81

Cindy Sampson (Lisa Braeden)....................................82

Nicholas Elia (Ben Braeden).....................................83

Episode 13 – Ghostfacers..84

Episode 14 – Long-Distance Call................................86

Sterling K. Brown (Gordon Walker)...............................87

Richard Speight Jr (Trickster) 88

Episode 15 – Time is on My Side 89

Episode 16 – No Rest for the Wicked 91

Production, Crew and Writing 92

Supernatural Trivia 93

Introduction

Following on from our earlier two quiz books on *Supernatural* Seasons 1 and 2, Light Bulb Quizzes has researched and compiled another 500 questions about the popular TV series, this time all about Season 3.

In this season, Sam Winchester (Jared Padalecki) is desperate to track down the demon that holds Dean's (Jensen Ackles) contract and prevent his brother from going to hell.

As the series progresses, tensions rise as it looks increasingly unlikely that Dean can be released from his deal and each of the Winchester brothers has to come to terms with the unthinkable.

Due to the strike by the Writers Guild of America, *Supernatural* Season 3 contains only sixteen episodes and we have, therefore, included more questions about each episode – some of them classics.

Our aim at Light Bulb Quizzes is to revisit past seasons of *Supernatural* and remember all the elements that go to making the series so enduring and popular, from quality writing and production to the superb actors that bring the characters to life.

We hope that you will enjoy the third in our series of quiz books about *Supernatural* as we continue to take a nostalgic look back at the Winchester brothers' battle against demons, monsters, spirits and creatures of the night.

Light Bulb Quizzes

Written by fans, for fans

Questions

'You can't escape me, Dean. You're going to die and this is what you're going to become.'
~ Demon Dean Winchester

Episode 1 – The Magnificent Seven

1. At the beginning of the episode, what appears on screen?

2. What happens to the man putting out the rubbish?

3. What does Bobby say to Sam on the phone?

4. When Dean, Sam and Bobby enter the farmhouse what do they find?

5. Who also turns up at the house?

6. What is the cause of death of the family?

7. Who is watching the house?

8. What does the man say to the woman in the clothes shop?

9. What effect does this have on the lady?

10. Who is following Sam?

11. What is 'John Doe's' real name?

12. Who turns up at the bar where the boys are tailing Walter?

13. What does one of the demons get Isaac to do?

14. How many demons are there and who are they?

15. What film is Dean quoting from when he says 'what's in the box'?

16. Which demon/sin was responsible for the death of the family that Dean, Sam and Bobby found?

17. Which demon/sin was responsible for the death of the female shopper?

18. Which one of the deadly sins tries to seduce Dean – Envy, Pride or Lust?

19. Who rescues Sam from Pride and the other demons?

20. What special weapon does she possess?

Episode 2 – The Kids are Alright

21. What happens to the dad in the beginning of the episode?

22. What is Dean's 'dying wish'?

23. Whose birthday party does Dean walk in on?

24. How old is Ben – eight, nine or ten?

25. What is striking about Ben?

26. What does the woman at the birthday party say about her daughter?

27. Who surprises Sam at the diner?

28. What reason does the above give for following Sam?

29. True or false: Since the Yellow-eyed demon died, Sam is no longer having visions?

30. Who is watching the sleeping woman?

31. What happens when the woman sees her daughter's reflection in the mirror?

32. What does Sam notice at the back of Dakota's mum's neck?

33. How does Katie's mother try to get rid of her 'daughter'?

34. Who is waiting for Katie's mother in her house when she gets home?

35. What are the Winchester brothers hunting?

36. What do the above feed on?

37. How do you kill this type of monster?

38. What happens when the mother changeling is killed?

39. The blonde woman asks Sam to check up on his mother's friends, what does he discover?

40. Who is the mystery woman and what does she say she can do for Sam?

Jensen Ackles (Dean Winchester)

41. Who is Jensen's all-time favourite musician?

42. What character does Jensen play in the 2007 independent romantic comedy movie *Ten Inch Hero*?

43. True or false: Jensen's hobbies include horse riding?

44. What is Jensen's favourite food?

45. In what play did Jensen appear on stage in Texas with Lou Diamond Phillips in 2007?

46. Jensen is more commonly a surname and is the most popular last name in which north European country?

47. Jensen was cast in the remake of which cult movie, filmed during the summer of 2008?

48. Jensen is good friends with which American country singer and actor?

49. Who was the first artist that Jensen saw in concert?

50. What creative pastime does Jensen enjoy – painting, writing poetry or photography?

Jared Padalecki (Sam Winchester)

51. In which Texas state was Jared born in 1982 – Austin, San Antonio or Houston?

52. What board game is Jared known to be skilled at?

53. What are Jared's parents' names?

54. Jared is good friends with which well-known *One Tree Hill* actor?

55. Can you name Jared's two dogs that he rescued from a shelter in the early years of *Supernatural*?

56. At what age did Jared begin taking acting classes?

57. What is Jared's mother's profession?

58. For which episode of *Supernatural* Season 3 did Jared do uncredited stunt work?

59. In what horror movie, released in February 2009, did Jared play the role of Clay Miller?

60. True or false: Jared got engaged to his long-term girlfriend, Sandra McCoy, in January 2008?

Episode 3 – Bad Day at Black Rock

61. Who visits Gordon Walker in prison?

62. Who does Gordon tell his friend must die?

63. The person calling on John Winchester's old phone warns Dean and Sam that something belonging to their father has been broken into, what is it?

64. What do Dean and Sam find there?

65. What is missing?

66. What does the missing box contain – a frog's head, a rabbit's foot or a unicorn horn?

67. In what way is Wayne lucky when a neighbour turns up?

68. Who grabs the rabbit's foot – Dean or Sam?

69. What does Dean get Sam to do while he is being 'lucky'?

70. What happens to the previous holder of the rabbit's foot?

71. What do Dean and Sam win for being Biggerson's one millionth customers?

72. How is a lucky rabbit's foot created?

73. How much money do Dean and Sam win on scratch cards – $10,000, $15,000 or $20,000?

74. Who steals the rabbit's foot?

75. What happens to Sam's shoe?

76. Who is the 'waitress' really?

77. What is Bela's profession?

78. How did Bela locate the rabbit's foot?

79. Who gives Dean and Sam the ritual to destroy the rabbit's foot?

80. True or false: Kubrick believes that God wants him to kill Dean?

Episode 4 – Sin City

81. In what town in Ohio is this episode set?

82. Where is the first scene set?

83. What does Andy say about God?

84. Where does the barmaid take Richie?

85. True or false: The barmaid is possessed by a demon?

86. How does Richie die?

87. What is Bobby working on?

88. Who offers to help him fix it?

89. How does Dean trap Casey, the barmaid?

90. Who does Casey say is God of the demons?

91. According to Casey, what does the name Lucifer mean?

92. What is the story behind the fall of Lucifer?

93. Who is being possessed by a centuries old demon – Bobby Singer, Father Gil or Trotter?

94. How does Casey describe hell?

95. What is the Yellow-eyed demon's real name?

96. Who was next in line to command the demon army?

97. Who turns up to save the day?

98. Which demon visits Sam at the end of the episode?

99. Who is concerned that Sam is 'not quite right'?

100. Why doesn't Sam kill Ruby?

Episode Titles

101. What episode takes its name from a crime thriller book and film of the same title?

102. What episode is named after a song by American rock singer, Alice Cooper?

103. Episode 10 'Dream a Little Dream of Me' takes its name from a 1931 song that was famously covered in 1968 by which American folk rock group?

104. What episode relates to the humanitarian side of battle; the 'law of waging war'?

105. What episode is named after a 1960 American western film?

106. Episode 15 'Time is on My Side' comes from a song written by Jeremy Ragovoy and made famous by which British rock band in 1964?

107. What episode title is based on a 1486 treatise on the prosecution of witches and literally translates to 'Hammer of Witches'?

108. Episode 3 'Bad Day at Black Rock' is named after a 1955 movie starring which American actor from the Golden Age of Hollywood?

109. Episode 2 'The Kids are Alright' takes its name from a song by which legendary British rock band?

110. British rock singer Ozzy Osbourne recorded an album with the same name as which episode?

Name the Episode

Can you name each of the following episodes from the plot summary?

111. Dean and Sam encounter Bela Talbot for the first time. Sam experiences some bad luck. Gordon Walker is in prison and plots to kill Sam with the hunter Kubrik.

112. The Winchester brothers are arrested. Viktor Henriksen is forced to believe in the existence of demons. Nancy volunteers to save them all from the siege. Dean and Sam walk away and Lilith kills everyone left behind.

113. A ghost ship appears to those with family blood on their hands. Gertrude Case takes a liking for Sam. Bela tricks Dean but then needs the Winchester brothers' help.

114. Dean and Sam take on Lilith. Bobby and Ruby both lend a hand. A family is terrorised by their possessed young daughter. Dean is dragged to hell.

115. Dean visits an old flame and meets a young version of himself. Sam meets Ruby in a diner. The Winchester brothers investigate a changeling and save the children of Cicero.

116. Victims are being kidnapped and having body parts removed. Bobby tracks down Bela. Someone wants Sam's eyes. Hellhounds are after Bela.

117. Dean and Sam are hunting a vampire. Gordon is turned into a monster. Sam saves Dean and garrottes Gordon. Dean teaches Sam how to fix the Impala.

118. The Winchester brothers investigate unusual deaths in Ohio. Casey reveals the Yellow-eyed demon's real name. Ruby tells Sam that she can help him to release Dean from his deal.

119. Ed Zeddmore and Harry Spengler show up. Dean, Sam and the investigators become trapped in a creepy old house with death echoes. Corbett is killed at a macabre birthday party. Sam is next, unless Dean can save him.

120. Dean and Sam come up against a coven of witches. Dean is the victim of a hex bag and is saved by an unlikely ally. Ruby admits to Dean that she can't save him.

Episode 5 – Bedtime Stories

121. How many brothers are at the building site in the first scene – two, three or four?

122. What do Dean and Sam initially think they may be hunting?

123. Who do the Winchester brothers interview at the hospital?

124. What do the couple who are lost in the woods discover?

125. What happens to the couple?

126. Who is watching the scene?

127. How does the female survivor of the attack describe the girl?

128. What does Sam think links the murders?

129. What animal do Dean and Sam see on the path – a cat, a mouse or a frog?

130. What is the next fairy tale to be referenced?

131. Who has chained up the young woman that Dean and Sam find in the house?

132. Who is at the scene, watching?

133. When the girl vanishes, what is left behind in her place?

134. What character from a fairy tale does the above relate to?

135. What is Dr Garrison reading to his daughter, Callie, who is in a coma in hospital?

136. Why is Callie in a coma?

137. Who is behind all of the mysterious deaths?

138. Where does Sam go at the end of the episode?

139. What does Sam ask her to do?

140. When she says this is not possible, what is Sam's response?

Episode 6 – Red Sky at Morning

141. What does the jogger see that is unusual?

142. What happens to the above in the shower?

143. Why is Dean arguing with Sam in the Impala?

144. True or false: Dean been released from his deal?

145. Who does Miss Case think the Winchester brothers are working with?

146. The ghost ship appears every 35, 37 or 39 years?

147. Which legendary ghost ship is referenced in this episode?

148. Who has Dean's car towed away?

149. How does the next victim die?

150. What do the victims have in common?

151. Who does the next victim see in his car before he too is drowned?

152. What is the ghost ship called?

153. What was cut from the ghost sailor after he died?

154. How can Dean and Sam destroy the above?

155. Who is Bela's date for the night – Dean or Sam?

156. Who is the other Winchester brother's date?

157. Who steals the Hand of Glory from Dean?

158. Who is the next victim to see the ghost ship?

159. What is the sailor spirit's motive?

160. What spirit do Dean and Sam summon in order to save Bela?

Supernatural Quotes

161. Fill in the blank from this quote by Bobby Singer, episode 1 'the Magnificent Seven' – 'Fat, drunk and ____ is no way to go through life son.'

162. Which Season 3 character's job is to 'procure unique items for a select clientèle'?

163. Who tells Sam 'Sometimes you just gotta let people go'?

164. Which character says, 'I had a type – leather jacket, couple of scars, no mailing address'?

165. Who describes themselves as 'that little fallen angel on your [Sam's] shoulder'?

166. Which 'sin' describes Dean as 'a walking billboard of gluttony and lust' in episode 1 'The Magnificent Seven'?

167. 'I smell good don't I? I taste even better' is a quote by Dean, Sam or Bobby?

168. Complete the quote by Ruby in episode 16 'No Rest for the Wicked'– 'you're almost hell's ____ '.

169. Which character says, 'When this is over, I'm gonna have so much sex'?

170. Which character says: 'Sometimes the spirit world is in a chatty mood, sometimes it isn't'?

Cast Appearances

171. What well-known teen drama series did actor Dustin Milligan, who plays Corbett in episode 13 'Ghostfacers', appear in as Ethan Ward in 2008–9?

172. Can you name the American actor who plays Kubrick in episode 3 'Bad Day at Black Rock' and episode 7 'Fresh Blood'?

173. Jared Padalecki's long-term girlfriend at the time, Sandra 'Sandy' McCoy, plays what role in episode 4 'Bedtime Stories'?

174. Can you name the American actress who has worked in the entertainment business for over forty years, who plays Gertrude Case in episode 6 'Red Sky at Morning'?

175. Actress Rachel Pattee plays Lilith in episode 12 'Jus in Bello'. Can you name the TV movie that she appeared in as Becky McAdams in 2008?

176. What actor who has appeared in *Desperate Housewives, 21 Jump Street* (TV series) and *Hill Street Blues,* plays the role of Rufus Turner in episode 15 'Time is on My Side'?

177. Actress Kristin Booth who plays Renee Van Allen in episode 9 'Malleus Maleficarum' starred in which 2003 movie with Ryan Reynolds?

178. Can you name third generation American actor who plays Edward Carrigan in episode 8 'A Very Supernatural Christmas'?

179. Which model and actress plays the role of Casey in episode 4 'Sin City'?

180. Anjul Nigem who plays Stewie Myers in episode 14 'Long-Distance Call' also appeared in several series of which popular medical drama series?

181. What actress plays the role of Lilith in episode 16 'No Rest for the Wicked'?

182. Can you name the actress of Mexican and Puerto Rican descent who, appeared in the American comedy series *George Lopez* as Veronica Palmero and plays Nancy in episode 12 'Jus in Bello'?

183. Actress Cherilyn Wilson who plays Lanie is episode 14 'Long-Distance Call' went on to appear in several episodes of which Beverly Hills based TV drama series?

184. Can you name the actress who plays Madge Carrigan in episode 8 'A Very Supernatural Christmas'?

185. Actress Marisa Ramirez who plays Tammi in episode 9 'Malleus Maleficarum' also appeared in 13 episodes of which American TV series about a psychiatrist?

Episode 7 – Fresh Blood

186. Who sneaks up on Bela in the first scene?

187. Where is he meant to be?

188. What does he take out of Bela's car without her knowledge?

189. What does he want to know?

190. What does he call Sam Winchester?

191. What does Bela want in exchange for revealing Dean and Sam's whereabouts?

192. What are Dean and Sam hunting?

193. How does Dean lure it out of hiding?

194. What does Dean inject the vampire with?

195. What is weird about Lucy?

196. What has happened to her?

197. Who do Dean and Sam run into whilst hunting?

198. Where does Gordon wake up?

199. What does the vampire, Dixon, do to Gordon?

200. Who finds Gordon for Dean and Sam?

201. What did Gordon do to the other two vampires in the nest?

202. Who does Gordon kill?

203. What happens to Dean and Sam?

204. True or false: Dean shoots the vampire with a bullet from the Colt?

205. What happens to Gordon?

Episode 8 – A Very Supernatural Christmas

206. What happens to the granddad at the beginning of the episode?

207. What does Sam find in the chimney?

208. What do Dean and Sam think they might be hunting?

209. What is the link between the two victims?

210. Why doesn't Sam want to celebrate Christmas?

211. What does (folk)lore say about the anti-Claus?

212. What does Sam ask the victim's wife and why?

213. What are the brothers really hunting?

214. True or false: The plant in the wreaths is meadowsweet?

215. What effect does this plant have?

216. What happens when you offer sacrifices to this pagan god?

217. Why does Dean want to celebrate Christmas this particular year?

218. What can kill a pagan god?

219. What do Dean and Sam find in Madge and Edward Carrigan's basement?

220. Who are the above couple?

221. What do the Carrigans do to Sam?

222. What happens during the ritual before the Carrigans can pull out one of Dean's teeth?

223. Where do Dean and Sam get more Everdeen stakes from?

224. In the flashback, what does young Sam give to young Dean as a Christmas present – a hunting journal, an amulet or a Barbie doll?

225. Sam prepares a surprise 'last Christmas' for Dean, can you name the things he does?

Katie Cassidy (Ruby)

226. Katie is the daughter of which famous pop star from the 1970s?

227. Which of the above pop star's songs did Katie cover?

228. In what year was Katie born – 1986, 1988 or 1990?

229. What are Katie's two middle names?

230. Which famous actress is Katie named after?

231. What 2008 action thriller movie, starring Liam Neeson, did Katie appear in as Amanda?

232. Can you name Katie's mother and her profession?

233. True or false: Katie is skilled at playing the drums and trumpet?

234. In which horror film did Katie make her movie debut in 2006?

235. How many episodes of *Supernatural* Season 3 does Katie appear in?

Lauren Cohen (Bela Talbot)

236. In what country was Lauren born – Canada, England or the US?

237. True or false: Lauren studied Drama and English Literature at Winchester University in the UK?

238. What role in *Supernatural* did Lauren originally audition for?

239. In what year was Lauren born?

240. What nationality is Lauren's mother?

241. In what 2005 movie starring Heath Ledger and Sienna Miller did Lauren appear as Sister Beatrice?

242. What combat sport does Lauren enjoy?

243. When not filming in the US, Lauren has a house in which European city?

244. What career did Lauren originally intend to follow if her modelling and acting career did not work out?

245. How many episodes of *Supernatural* Season 3 does Lauren's character Bela Talbot appear in?

Episode 9 – Malleus Maleficarum

246. What happens to the woman in the bathroom in the first scene?

247. Who discovers the hex bag in the above victim's apartment?

248. Who or what is responsible for the victim, Janet's death?

249. According to Sam, why is it difficult to track down a witch?

250. What does Amanda take out of her oven?

251. What item belonging to the victim, Paul, does Amanda use for her spell?

252. Who saves Paul when he chokes on a maggot infested burger

253. Who is the next victim to die?

254. What does Dean walk into in Amanda's kitchen that upsets him?

255. What is the coven of witches working under the guise of?

256. What book do the witches kneel before?

257. What is growing in Elizabeth's 'victory garden'?

258. Who stops Dean and Sam in the Impala?

259. Why is Dean concerned about Sam?

260. Who is the witches' next victim?

261. Which member of the coven is really a demon – Renee, Elizabeth or Tammi?

262. True or false: When she was human, Ruby was a witch?

263. Who uses Ruby's knife to kill the demon?

264. How does Ruby describe hell to Dean

265. Why does Ruby want Dean's help?

Episode 10 – Dream a Little Dream of Me

266. Who is attacked in the old house in the opening sequence?

267. Who is drinking whiskey alone in a bar at 2.00 p.m. in the afternoon?

268. Bobby is in hospital in a coma, where does Sam find details of the case he was working on?

269. What was Dr Greggs investigating before he died?

270. Who does Dean go to interview?

271. What sleep disorder is the student suffering from – sleep apnoea, Charcot-Wilbrand syndrome or insomnia?

272. What did the doctor give the student to help?

273. Can you name the plant that the doctor was using?

274. According to legend, what is the above plant used for?

275. What does Dean suggest that he and Sam do?

276. Who do Dean and Sam ask to get them the African Dream Root?

277. What does Sam add to the Dream Root potion?

278. Where do Dean and Sam wake up in their dream?

279. True or false: Bobby killed his wife?

280. Who attacks Sam in the dream garden?

281. What happened to Jeremy as a child that caused him to stop dreaming?

282. Who does Dean see on a picnic in his next dream?

283. Who is Dean forced to confront in the bedroom?

284. Who does Sam bring into the dream to stop Jeremy?

285. What does Bela steal from the Winchester brothers at the end of the episode?

Supernatural Soundtrack

286. What song does Sam repeatedly wake up to on a Tuesday in episode 11 'Mystery Spot'?

287. What song plays in the above episode when Sam finally wakes up on Wednesday?

288. How many Season 3 episodes do not feature a soundtrack?

289. 'You Ain't Seen Nothing Yet' by Bachman-Turner Overdrive features in which episode?

290. What 'party' song is playing in the basement in episode 13 'Ghostfacers'?

291. What song by Creedence Clearwater Revival features in episode 3 'Sin City' – 'Bad Moon Rising', 'Proud Mary' or 'Run through the Jungle'?

292. What song is being played at Ben's birthday party in episode 2 'The Kids are Alright'?

293. 'I Put a Spell on You' by Screamin' Jay Hawkins features in which episode?

294. What song is playing at the end of episode 8 'A Very Supernatural Christmas' when Dean and Sam exchange gifts?

295. What song do Dean and Sam sing along to (very badly) in the Impala on the way to kill Lilith in episode 16 'No Rest for the Wicked'?

Monsters and Demons

296. Name the mythical creature from India that can take on human form and suck out a person's soul?

297. Can you name the demon with white eyes that was the first to be created and was once human?

298. Which Season 3 monster assumes the identity of a child, but feeds on the mother?

299. What are a group of witches known as?

300. What is a death omen in *Supernatural*?

301. Hold Nikar are a type of what?

302. In popular folklore is a rabbit's foot supposed to bring good or bad luck?

303. What immortal creature revels in causing mischief?

304. What are a group of vampires called in *Supernatural*?

305. What is the name of a collection of supernatural ingredients, including an item belonging to the victim, wrapped in cloth and bound with leather used by witches to harm others?

Episode 11 – Mystery Spot

306. What day of the week is it in this episode – Tuesday, Wednesday or Thursday?

307. What was the 'special' breakfast in the diner?

308. What happens to Dean?

309. What happens to Sam?

310. What does Sam think has happened?

311. What happens to Dean next time?

312. What happens to Sam again?

313. What does Dean order at the diner instead of bacon and what happens to him?

314. How many Tuesdays does Sam say they have lived through?

315. What does Sam start doing to prove his story to Dean?

316. What does the man at the counter do differently the next time round?

317. Why does Sam say that is weird?

318. True or false: A trickster is behind the reoccurring Tuesdays?

319. Who is all of this for?

320. What happens when Sam wakes up the next day?

321. What happens to Dean?

322. What occurs over the next six months as shown in the montage?

323. What does Bobby find to help Sam?

324. What does Sam promise the trickster?

325. What does the Trickster tell Sam his weakness is?

Episode 12 – Jus in Bello

326. Whose hotel room are Dean and Sam searching at the beginning of the episode?

327. Who charges into the room and why?

328. What does the (demon) FBI Deputy Director do to Dean and Sam?

329. What happens when one of the FBI agents tries to talk to Bill on the walkie talkie?

330. Who does the FBI think is behind the 'siege'?

331. What does Sam take from Nancy other than the towel?

332. What does FBI agent Victor Henriksen do to the police sheriff?

333. Why does he do this?

334. What does Dean see when getting weapons out of his trunk?

335. What does Dean do to prevent the people in the station being possessed by demons – gives them protective charms, douses them in holy water or draws an anti-possession tattoo on them?

336. What does Nancy Fitzgerald see outside the window?

337. What does the sergeant accidently break?

338. Who breaks in through the back window?

339. Who has sent the demons to surround the station?

340. True or false: Nancy offers to sacrifice herself in a spell to obliterate the demons?

341. What else does she need in order for the spell to work?

342. Who is the only person they can use?

343. What is Dean's plan?

344. When the demons are trapped inside, what do Dean and Sam do?

345. What happens at the station after Dean and Sam have left?

Cindy Sampson (Lisa Braeden)

346. What nationality is Cindy – American, Canadian or British?

347. What Canadian television series did Cindy appear in as Sandra MacLaren in 2006–7?

348. What is Cindy's middle name?

349. In what year was Cindy born?

350. True or false: Cindy attended the Randolph Academy of Performing Arts in Toronto?

351. What 2006 American comedy movie did Cindy appear in with Ben Affleck's brother, Casey?

352. What role did Cindy play in the 2009 Canadian TV series *Durham County*?

353. What role in *Supernatural* did Cindy originally audition for?

354. What is the first episode of *Supernatural* that Cindy's character, Lisa, appears in?

355. How many episodes of *Supernatural* did Cindy go on to appear in as Lisa Braeden?

Nicholas Elia (Ben Braeden)

356. In what year was Nicholas born – 1995, 1997 or 1999?

357. What nationality is Nicholas?

358. What 2005 supernatural thriller movie did Nicholas appear in as Mike Rivers?

359. What character did Nicholas play in the 2008 movie *Speed Racer* starring Susan Sarandon?

360. Nicholas appeared in what 2007 movie starring Jason Statham?

361. Nicholas appeared in which 2007 American drama movie starring Sharon Stone?

362. What is Nicholas's *Supernatural* character's full name?

363. How old is Ben Braeden when Dean first meets him?

364. What relation is Nicholas's character, Ben, to Dean Winchester?

365. In what year was Ben Braeden born in *Supernatural*?

Episode 13 – Ghostfacers

366. Who do we see at the beginning of the episode?

367. What is the name of the supernatural reality TV programme they are filming?

368. Who are the other three members of the team?

369. What are they investigating?

370. What is command centre one?

371. Can you name the three phases of the investigation as identified by the *Ghostfacers'* team?

372. What scares Harry in the house – a ghost, a dead rat or a live pigeon?

373. Who do Ed and his friend, Corbett, bump into?

374. What do Harry and the team see in the house?

375. What happens to people who stay in the house overnight?

376. What do Dean and Sam call the vison of the man's death?

377. Who gets taken first?

378. What happens after the person above gets taken?

379. True or false: A hospital janitor was the last owner of the house?

380. What does Dean find in a case in one of the rooms?

381. Who is the next person to disappear?

382. What happens to Corbett?

383. What does Dean tell the remaining members of the team to do?

384. Whose death echo do they see being replayed over and over again?

385. What happens at the end of the episode?

Episode 14 – Long-Distance Call

386. Why is the man [Ben] in the first sequence distressed?

387. What does Ben do to the phone?

388. What happens next?

389. In the next scene, Dean and Sam are arguing, what does Sam want to do?

390. Dean and Sam interview Ben's wife, what does she say was unusual about Ben's phone call?

391. What is the phone number and what is unusual about it?

392. How many other houses have been receiving calls from the above number – five, ten or twenty?

393. Who speaks to Sam about calls that they have been receiving?

394. Who has the above been talking to on the phone?

395. Who phones Dean?

396. What do Dean and Sam go to investigate at the museum?

397. What message is repeated over and over on Lanie's computer screen?

398. What does John Winchester tell Dean about in his next phone call?

399. Who is the next person to receive a ghostly phone call?

400. What monster are Dean and Sam hunting?

401. Whose identity has the above taken on?

402. Who phones the next victim?

403. Who does she say killed her?

404. Who tracks down the crocotta and kills it?

405. What does Dean admit to Sam at the end of the episode?

Sterling K. Brown (Gordon Walker)

406. Sterling attended Stanford University, where he studied drama, but what subject was he originally planning to major in?

407. True or false: Sterling has a Master's in Fine Arts from Tisch School of the Arts, New York University?

408. Which actress did Sterling marry in 2007?

409. What American television series did Sterling appear in as Roland Burton 2007–13?

410. In what American crime thriller movie starring Robert de Niro and Al Pacino did Sterling play the character Rogers in 2008?

411. Sterling and his wife had their first child in 2012, a son or daughter?

412. In which comedy television series did Sterling play the role of Adam Williams?

413. In 2004 Sterling appeared as Kelvin George in which television police drama in an episode titled 'Chatty Chatty Bang Bang'?

414. What kind of creature is Sterling's *Supernatural* character, Gordon Walker, obsessed with hunting?

415. How many episodes of *Supernatural* does Gordon Walker appear in?

Richard Speight Jr (Trickster)

416. In what year was Richard born in Nashville, Tennessee?

417. Who in Richard's life are Barby and Lindy?

418. What character did Richard play in the American post-apocalyptic series *Jericho* in 2006–8 – Dick, Bill or Jimmy?

419. Richard married Jaci Hays in 2003, how many children do the couple have?

420. True or false: Richard works as an emcee for Salute to *Supernatural* events organised by Creation Entertainment?

421. Richard provided the voice for Private Stephen Kelly for which well-known video game in 2005?

422. In which 2001 television series did Richard play the role of Sergeant Warren 'Skip' Muck?

423. How old was Richard when he started dancing lessons – five, seven or nine?

424. What is the name of the band that Richard used to belong to?

425. In what thriller movie did Richard appear in 2006?

Episode 15 – Time is on My Side

426. What happens to the man we see at the beginning of the episode?

427. What are Dean and Sam doing and why?

428. What is found on the victim's body?

429. Why is this interesting to Dean and Sam?

430. What do Dean and Sam think they are hunting?

431. What does the doctor say happened to the man's liver?

432. What body part is removed from the next victim – heart, lung or kidney?

433. Where had they heard of a similar case beforehand?

434. What is taken from the next victim?

435. Who calls Bobby with information about Bela?

436. Why was Sam interested in this particular case?

437. With what does Dean bribe Rufus so that he will help him – a bottle of whisky, a bottle of rum or a bottle of brandy?

438. What does Sam find in the cabin in the woods?

439. What does Dean find out about Bela Talbot?

440. What does Dean notice above Bela's door?

441. What body part does the Doc want to take from Sam – his ears, his eyes or his teeth?

442. How do Dean and Sam kill the Doc?

443. True or false: As a teenager Bela made a deal with a demon?

444. Who holds both Bela's and Dean's contracts?

445. What happens to Bela at the end of the episode?

Episode 16 – No Rest for the Wicked

446. In his dream, what is Dean running from at the beginning of the episode?

447. When Dean is hallucinating, what does he see Sam's face transform into?

448. What does Sam suggest to help them find Lilith?

449. What does Sam do against Dean's wishes?

450. What does Sam want from her?

451. What does she tell Sam?

452. What does she tell Sam is dormant?

453. How does Dean get the knife?

454. What does Dean put on the ceiling?

455. What does Dean tell Sam his weak spot is?

456. What does Pat give Dom?

457. On the way to Lilith, Dean, Sam and Bobby are pulled over by a policer officer, possessed by a demon, how does Dean know what it is?

458. True or false: The little girl kills her granddad?

459. Who is possessing the little girl – Ruby or Lilith?

460. What does Bobby do to the water supply?

461. Who attacks Dean?

462. What happens when Sam goes to kill the little girl?

463. Who does Lilith possess next?

464. Who does she let in?

465. Where is Dean at the end of the episode?

Production, Crew and Writing

466. What writer, who joined *Supernatural* during Season 3, writing four episodes, was responsible for the script for episode 8 'A Very Supernatural Christmas'?

467. Who is *Supernatural*'s stunt co-ordinator?

468. Series producer Robert Singer directed three episodes of *Supernatural* Season 3, can you name them?

469. Can you name the talented writer and producer who wrote five episodes of *Supernatural* Season 3 including episode 12 'Jus in Bello'?

470. Who is *Supernatural*'s director of photography?

471. How many episodes of Season 3 did *Supernatural* series creator Eric Kripke write?

472. Which multi-award nominated episode did director Philip Sgriccia, who has been with *Supernatural* since the first series, direct?

473. Can you name the respected and much-loved executive producer on *Supernatural* who directed four episodes of Season 3?

474. Ben Edlund wrote three episodes of Season 3, episode 3 'Bad Day at Black Rock', episode 9 'Malleus Maleficarum' and which other episode?

475. Which *Supernatural* producer and director wrote episode 4 'Sin City'?

Supernatural Trivia

476. Can you name all the ways mentioned that Dean dies in episode 11 'Mystery Spot'?

477. In which Season 3 episode of *Supernatural* is the Yellow-eyed demon's real name revealed?

478. What is the Yellow-eyed demon's name?

479. Which actor was nominated for a 2008 Young Artist Award for Best Performance in a TV Series?

480. What is the name of the fictitious porn site, favoured by Dean, and referenced in episode 14 'Long-Distance Call' that recurs throughout *Supernatural*?

481. What famous character from a 1960 Alfred Hitchcock movie does Sam refer to in episode 13 'Ghostfacers'?

482. In what month during 2007 was *Supernatural Magazine* launched by Titan Magazines?

483. For what SFX award was Jensen Ackles nominated in 2007 and Jared Padalecki in 2008?

484. Six fairy tales are referenced in episode 5 'Bedtime Stories', how many can you name?

485. What 1999 horror movie about three students is referenced in episode 9 'Malleus Maleficarum'?

486. Which episode of *Supernatural* Season 3 was nominated for several Primetime Emmy awards in various categories including Foley artist, music editor and sound effects editor?

487. What Canadian university do Dean and Sam visit in episode 14 'Long-Distance Call' to see Thomas Edison's 'ghost' phone?

488. To whom is Dean referring in episode 15 'Time is on My Side' when he mentions 'Sid and Nancy'?

489. Can you name the motel that Dean and Sam stay at in episode 15 'Time is on My Side', set in Erie, Pennsylvania?

490. In which Season 3 episode do Dean and Sam reveal their tattoos to ward off demons?

491. In episode 4 'Sin City', Casey says that she makes 'a mean hurricane' – a cocktail, made up of which ingredients?

492. Which 1967 album by British band The Beatles is referenced by Bela in episode 10 'Dream a Little Dream of Me'?

493. Which *Mary Poppins* actor who played a chimney sweep is mentioned by Sam in episode 8 'A Very Supernatural Christmas'?

494. Can you name the pub where the deadly sins demons meet up in episode 1 'The Magnificent Seven'?

495. Which 1993 movie starring Bill Murray is referenced in episode 11 'Mystery Spot'?

496. Sam's rental car in episode 15 'Time is on My Side' was from Lariat Car Rentals, the same company used in which paranormal TV drama series?

497. The character Kubrick shares his name with a famous director, can you name him?

498. Which victim in episode 7 'True Blood' shares a Christian name with one of *Dracula*'s victims in the novel by Bram Stoker?

499. In what Season 3 episode are we introduced to Ruby's demon killing knife?

500. Why are there only 16 episodes of *Supernatural* Season 3?

Answers

'Keep fighting, take care of my wheels, remember what Dad taught you, and remember what I taught you.'

~ Dean Winchester

Episode 1 – The Magnificent Seven

1. A dark black cloud
2. He forcefully inhales thick black smoke and is possessed by a demon
3. That he has finally found signs of demon activity
4. A dead family rotting on the sofa in front of the television
5. Tamara and Isaac, a husband and wife hunting team
6. Dehydration and starvation
7. A blonde woman
8. 'Man those are nice shoes' (pointing to another woman)
9. She immediately wants the shoes and when she finds out they are the last pair, she smashes the woman's face on the windscreen of a car outside the shop, killing her.
10. The same blonde that was outside the house
11. Walter Rosen: The first victim to be possessed by one of the sin demons
12. Tamara and Isaac
13. Drink a bottle of bleach
14. Seven: the Seven Deadly Sins (as documented in *Binsfeld's Classification of Demons*)
15. *Seven*
16. Sloth
17. Envy

18. Lust

19. The blonde woman

20. A knife that kills demons

Episode 2 – The Kids are Alright

21. The power saw turns itself on, he falls on to the moving saw and dies

22. To go to Cicero to visit Lisa Braeden, a girl that he once spent a weekend with

23. That of Lisa's son, Ben

24. Eight

25. He is like a 'mini-me' of Dean

26. There is something wrong with her and she is not really her daughter

27. The mysterious blonde woman from the previous episode

28. Sam is the only survivor of the Yellow-eyed demon's psychic kids

29. True

30. Her daughter, Katie

31. She sees a monster instead of her daughter's reflection

32. A strange bruise-like mark

33. She locks her in the car and leaves the hand brake off, so the car runs into a lake

34. Katie (dripping wet)

35. A changeling

36. The mother of the child they have taken over

37. Burn them

38. All the other changelings go up in flames too

39. They are all dead
40. A demon, she can save Dean

Jensen Ackles (Dean Winchester)

41. Garth Brooks
42. Priestly
43. True
44. Steak
45. *A Few Good Men*
46. Denmark
47. *My Bloody Valentine 3D*
48. Christian Kane
49. Michael Jackson
50. Photography

Jared Padalecki (Sam Winchester)

51. San Antonio
52. Chess
53. Gerald (Gerry) and Sherri
54. Chad Michael Murray
55. Sadie and Harley (Harley passed away in 2011)
56. Twelve-years-old
57. Teacher
58. Episode 4 'Sin City'
59. *Friday the 13th*
60. True: The couple ended their relationship later the same year

Episode 3 – Bad Day at Black Rock

61. Kubrick, a hunter

62. Sam Winchester

63. A storage container

64. A devil's trap, a human trap, childhood memorabilia, weapons and curse boxes

65. One of the curse boxes (a locked box covered in sigils)

66. A 'lucky' rabbit's foot

67. The neighbour used to be an army medic and he tends to Wayne's shotgun wound

68. Sam

69. Fill in scratch cards

70. He dies from slipping on a bottle and impaling himself on a barbeque skewer

71. Free food for one year

72. The foot must be cut off the rabbit in a cemetery under a full moon on Friday 13th

73. $15,000

74. A waitress

75. He gets gum on it and then it falls down a drain

76. Bela Talbot

77. She is a high class thief who sources supernatural objects for well-paying clients

78. By asking the ghosts of the people it had killed

79. Bobby Singer

80. False: He is on a mission from God to kill Sam, not Dean

Episode 4 – Sin City

81. Elizabethville

82. In a church

83. 'God's not with us anymore'

84. To an old mansion inherited from her parents

85. True

86. The possessed barmaid snaps his neck

87. Repairing the Colt and making more bullets for it

88. Ruby

89. By tracking Richie's GPS and drawing a demon trap on the floor of her basement

90. Lucifer

91. Light bringer

92. That he was the most beautiful of all God's angels, one day God demanded that he bow down before man and when he refused, God banished him

93. Father Gil

94. A pit of despair

95. Azazel

96. Sam Winchester

97. Bobby and Ruby, with the Colt

98. Ruby

99. Dean

100. She says that she can help Dean get out of his deal with the crossroads demon

Episode Titles

101. Episode 4 'Sin City'
102. Episode 7 'Fresh Blood'
103. The Mamas and the Papas
104. Episode 12 'Jus in Bello'
105. Episode 1 'The Magnificent Seven'
106. The Rolling Stones
107. Episode 9 'Malleus Maleficarum'
108. Spencer Tracy
109. The Who
110. Episode 16 'No Rest for the Wicked'

Name the Episode

111. Episode 3 'Bad Day at Black Rock'
112. Episode 12 'Jus in Bello'
113. Episode 6 'Red Sky at Morning'
114. Episode 16 'No Rest for the Wicked'
115. Episode 2 'The Kids are Alright'
116. Episode 15 'Time is on My Side'
117. Episode 7 'Fresh Blood'
118. Episode 4 'Sin City'
119. Episode 13 'Ghostfacers'
120. Episode 9 'Malleus Maleficarum'

Episode 5 – Bedtime Stories

121. Three

122. A werewolf

123. The only survivor of the first attack

124. A house occupied by an old lady

125. They are drugged and the old lady stabs the man to death

126. A young girl

127. Dark hair, pale skin, about eight, a beautiful child

128. Fairy tales

129. A frog

130. *Cinderella*

131. Her stepmother

132. The same young girl as before

133. A red apple

134. *Snow White*

135. *Grimm's Fairy Tales*

136. She was poisoned with bleach by her stepmother

137. Callie

138. To summon a crossroads demon

139. Release Dean from his deal

140. Sam kills the demon with the Colt

Episode 6 – Red Sky at Morning

141. A ghost ship

142. She is grabbed by a mysterious figure and drowned

143. Sam went after the Crossroads demon and wasted a bullet from the Colt

144. False

145. Alex

146. 37 years

147. *The Flying Dutchman*

148. Bela Talbot

149. He is drowned in the bath (by a mysterious figure)

150. They have all seen the ghost ship

151. The ghost of a sailor

152. *Espirito Santo*

153. His right hand, to make a Hand of Glory

154. Find it and burn it

155. Dean

156. Gert (Gertrude Case) the 70-year-old aunt of the first victim

157. Bela

158. Bela

159. Revenge: He goes after people who have killed a member of their family

160. The brother of the ghost sailor, who had him hung

Supernatural Quotes

161. Stupid
162. Bela Talbot (episode 3 'Bad Day at Black Rock')
163. The Trickster (episode 11 'Mystery Spot')
164. Lisa Braeden (episode 2 'The Kids are Alright')
165. Ruby (episode 4 'Sin City')
166. Envy
167. Dean (episode 7 'Fresh Blood')
168. Bitch
169. Nancy (episode 12 'Jus in Bello')
170. Bela Talbot (episode 10 'Dream a Little Dream')

Cast Appearances

171. *90210*

172. Michael Masse

173. A crossroads demon

174. Ellen Geer

175. *Twister Valley* (Originally *Tornado Valley*)

176. Steven Williams

177. *Foolproof*

178. Spencer Garrett

179. Sasha Barresse

180. *Grey's Anatomy*

181. Sierra McCormick

182. Aimee Garcia

183. *90210*

184. Merrilyn Gann

185. *Mental*

Episode 7 – Fresh Blood

186. Gordon Walker

187. In prison

188. Her gun

189. Where to find the Winchester brothers

190. The Antichrist

191. The (priceless) mojo bag around Gordon's waist

192. A vampire

193. By cutting his arm (so it can smell the blood)

194. Dead man's blood

195. She says she took something and can't come down (she doesn't know she has become a vampire)

196. A vampire put a couple drops of a 'drug' in her drink (but it was really vampire blood)

197. Gordon and Kubrick

198. Tied to a bed in the vampires' nest

199. Turn him into a vampire

200. Bela

201. Killed them – chopped off their heads

202. His hunting partner, Kubrick

203. They are separated trapping Sam with Gordon, who then turns out the lights

204. True

205. Sam kills him by strangling him with a wire and decapitating him

Episode 8 – A Very Supernatural Christmas

206. He gets pulled up the chimney and torn to shreds

207. A tooth

208. Evil Santa

209. They both visited the same place before they died – Santa's Village

210. Because he hasn't got very good memories of previous Christmases

211. That it'll walk with a limp and smell like sweets

212. Where she got the wreath above her fireplace because the other victim's house had the same one

213. Pagan gods of the winter solstice who grant clement weather

214. True

215. In pagan lore, meadowsweet is used in human sacrifice

216. It brings mild weather

217. Because it's his last year

218. An evergreen stake

219. Human remains; bones, blood, and a blood-soaked Santa costume

220. Hold Nickar – pagan gods

221. Pull out one of his fingernails

222. Someone rings on the doorbell

223. The Carrigans' Christmas tree

224. An amulet (that Dean has worn ever since) that he intended to give to his father, John

225. Decorates the hotel room with a tree hung with air fresheners, makes eggnog, buys him presents; oil for the Impala and a candy bar

Katie Cassidy (Ruby)

226. David Cassidy

227. I Think I Love You

228. 1986 (November)

229. Evelyn Anita

230. Katharine Hepburn

231. *Taken*

232. Sherry Williams; model, now actress

233. False: She plays guitar and piano

234. *When a Stranger Calls*

235. Six: episode 1 'The Magnificent Seven', episode 2 'The Kids are Alright', episode 4 'Sin City', episode 9 'Malleus Maleficarum', episode 12 'Jus in Bello' and episode 16 'No Rest for the Wicked'

Lauren Cohen (Bela Talbot)

236. The US (Cherry Hill, New Jersey)
237. True
238. Ruby
239. 1982
240. British (Scottish)
241. *Casanova*
242. Kickboxing
243. London
244. Child psychologist
245. Six: episode 3 'Bad Day at Black Rock', episode 6 'Red Sky at Morning', episode 7 'Fresh Blood', episode 10 'Dream a Little Dream of Me', episode 12 'Jus in Bello' and episode 15 'Time is on My Side'

Episode 9 – Malleus Maleficarum

246. Her teeth start to fall out and she chokes to death on her own blood
247. Sam
248. A witch
249. Witches are human and could be anyone
250. Rotten meat infested with maggots
251. His watch
252. The Winchester brothers
253. The witch, Amanda
254. A dead rabbit, strung up on a hook
255. A book club
256. *The Book of Shadows*
257. Belladonna, wolfsbane and mandrake
258. Ruby
259. Because he is acting out of character (cares less about killing people)
260. Dean
261. Tammi (Benton)
262. True
263. Dean
264. Losing your humanity and forgetting who you are
265. To prepare Sam to fight demons when Dean dies

Episode 10 – Dream a Little Dream of Me

266. Bobby Singer

267. Sam Winchester

268. In the closet in his motel room

269. Sleep disorders

270. One of Dr Gregg's research students

271. Charcot-Wilbrand syndrome (he is unable to dream)

272. Yellow tea

273. African Dream Root (*Silene capensis*)

274. Dream walking

275. Go dream walking (inside Bobby's head)

276. Bela

277. Bobby's hair

278. Bobby's house

279. True: Because she was possessed

280. Jeremy, the research student that Dean interviewed

281. His violent father hit him with a baseball bat

282. Lisa (Braeden)

283. Himself (demon Dean)

284. Jeremy's father

285. The Colt

Supernatural Soundtrack

286. 'Heat of the Moment' by Asia

287. 'Back in Time' by Huey Lewis and the News

288. Four: episode 5 'Bedtime Stories', episode 12 'Jus in Bello', episode 14 'Long-distance Call' and episode 15 'Time is on My Side'

289. Episode 1 'The Magnificent Seven' (plays when Sam discovers Dean with the twins)

290. 'It's My Party' by Leslie Gore

291. Run through the Jungle

292. 'Goodnight City' by 40.000 Miles

293. Episode 9 'Malleus Maleficarum'

294. 'Have Yourself a Merry Little Christmas' by Rosemary Clooney

295. 'Wanted Dead or Alive' by Bon Jovi

Monsters and Demons

296. Crocotta (episode 14 'Long Distance Call')

297. Lilith (episode 12 'Jus in Bello' and episode 16 'No Rest for the Wicked')

298. A changeling (episode 2 'The Kids are Alright')

299. A coven

300. An apparition of a deceased person that foretells of death (episode 13 'Ghostfacers')

301. Pagan god (episode 8 'A Very Supernatural Christmas')

302. Good luck (episode 3 'Bad Day at Black Rock')

303. A trickster (episode 11 'Mystery Spot')

304. A nest

305. Hex bag (episode 9 'Malleus Maleficarum')

Episode 11 – Mystery Spot

306. Tuesday

307. Pig 'n a poke

308. Dean gets shot by the owner of Mystery Spot and dies

309. Sam wakes up in the same place, at the same time, on Tuesday again, after Dean is shot

310. It was a dream

311. He gets hit by a car and dies all over again

312. He wakes up and it's Tuesday again, he thinks they are in a time loop

313. A sausage, he chokes on it and dies again

314. 100

315. Speaking the same words at the same time (because he knows what Dean is going to say)

316. He has strawberry syrup on his pancakes instead of maple

317. Because nothing in the diner ever changes, except him

318. True

319. For Sam, so that he will realise what it will be like when Dean dies and that he can't save him

320. It is Wednesday

321. He is held at gun point and shot dead

322. Sam goes on without Dean, hunting and killing monsters, but he withdraws into himself, doesn't return Bobby's calls and obsesses over the trickster

323. A summoning ritual, to summon the trickster

324. That if he takes him to next Wednesday, he won't come after him

325. Dean

Episode 12 – Jus in Bello

326. Bela's hotel room

327. The police/FBI because Bela tipped them off

328. Shoots at them, hitting Dean in the shoulder

329. The frequency is interrupted

330. Dean and Sam's friends who are going to try and bust them out

331. Her rosary (to put in the toilet to make holy water)

332. Shoots him in the head

333. He is possessed by a demon

334. A mass of black smoke (a hoard of demons) heading towards the station

335. He gives them protective charms

336. Numerous people possessed by demons surrounding the building

337. A salt line by the back window

338. Ruby

339. Lilith

340. False, Ruby offers to sacrifice herself

341. The heart of 'a person of virtue'; a virgin

342. Nancy

343. To open the doors, let the demons in and fight their way out

344. Play a recorded exorcism over the speakers

345. Lilith arrives and kills everyone in the station

Cindy Sampson (Lisa Braeden)

346. Canadian

347. *Rumours*

348. Marie

349. 1978

350. True

351. *The Last Kiss*

352. Molly Krocker

353. Bela Talbot

354. Season 3 episode 2 'The Kids are Alright'

355. Eleven

Nicholas Elia (Ben Braeden)

356. 1997

357. Canadian

358. *White Noise*

359. Young Speed Racer

360. *War*

361. *When a Man Falls in the Forest*

362. Benjamin Isaac Braeden

363. Eight, on his birthday

364. No relation, although Dean believes that Ben may be his son (Lisa denies this)

365. 1999 (May)

Episode 13 – Ghostfacers

366. Harry Spangler and Ed Zeddmore

367. *Ghostfacers*

368. Maggie Zeddmore (Ed's sister), Spruce and Corbett

369. A leap year ghost (that appears every four years) at Morton house

370. The eagle's nest

371. Phase I = Homework, Phase II = Infiltration and Phase III = Face time

372. A dead rat

373. Dean and Sam Winchester

374. An apparition of a man talking, who then gets shot in the chest and disappears

375. They die

376. A death echo

377. Corbett

378. The house locks all the exits, trapping the occupants inside

379. True: Freeman Daggett

380. Toe tags from corpses which match the people seen in the death echoes

381. Sam

382. He is killed by the ghost of Freeman Daggett

383. Take the salt from his bag, make a circle and stay inside

384. Corbett's

385. Dean and Sam watch *Ghostfacers* with the team but when they leave they erase the episode by using an electro magnet to wipe the computers

Episode 14 – Long-Distance Call

386. He keeps receiving phone calls from Linda, his old girlfriend who died in a car accident years ago

387. He smashes it and rips it out of the wall

388. The phone starts ringing and Ben puts a gun under his chin and shoots himself in the head

389. Summon Ruby

390. When she picked up another phone to listen in, there was no one on the other end of the line

391. SHA33: The number is over 100 years old

392. Ten

393. A young girl named Lanie (Greenfield)

394. Her mum, who died three years ago

395. His father, John Winchester (who gave his life in exchange for Dean's)

396. Thomas Edison's 'ghost' phone

397. Come to me

398. An exorcism to kill the demon holding his contract

399. Lanie's younger brother, Simon, on his toy phone

400. A crocotta

401. Clark Adams, the supervisor of the phone company

402. His nine-year-old daughter who was murdered

403. 'The man at the house' – Dean

404. Sam

405. That he is scared of going to hell

Sterling K. Brown (Gordon Walker)

406. Economics

407. True

408. Ryan Michelle Bathe

409. *Army Wives*

410. *Righteous Kill*

411. A son named Andrew

412. *Starved*

413. *NYPD Blue*

414. Vampires

415. Four: Season 2 episode 3 'Bloodlust' and episode 10 'Hunted'; Season 3 episode 3 'Bad Day at Black Rock' and episode 7 'Fresh Blood'

Richard Speight Jr (Trickster)

416. 1970

417. His two older sisters

418. Bill

419. Three sons: Steve, Fletcher and Frank

420. True

421. *Call of Duty 2* (and also *Call of Duty 2: Big Red One*)

422. *Band of Brothers*

423. Five-years-old

424. Fugitive Pope

425. *Open Water 2: Adrift*

Episode 15 – Time is on My Side

426. He is abducted and later arrives at the hospital begging for help (his liver has been cut out)

427. Torturing a demon with holy water to find out who holds the contract for Dean's soul

428. Bloody fingerprints that don't match his DNA

429. Because they belong to a man who died in 1981

430. A zombie

431. It was not ripped out, it was removed surgically

432. Kidney

433. From their father, John Winchester's journal. He had hunted a Doc Benton who was seeking immortality

434. His heart

435. Rufus Turner

436. Because he thinks that if Dean can find out how to live forever then he won't go to hell

437. A bottle of whisky (Johnnie Walker Blue Label)

438. The doctor's lair with a dead man strapped to a table and a live girl strapped to another table with a maggot-infested wound

439. That Bela (Abby) killed her parents at the age of 14 and inherited millions of dollars

440. Devil's shoestring to keeps hellhounds away

441. Eyes

442. They don't – they lock him in a chained, metal box and bury it deep underground

443. True

444. Lilith

445. She is taken by hellhounds

Episode 16 – No Rest for the Wicked

446. Hellhounds

447. A hellhound

448. That he summons Ruby

449. Summons Ruby

450. Her knife

451. That Lilith is on vacation and her guard is down

452. His psychic (demon) powers

453. During a fight with Ruby

454. A devil's trap, to trap Ruby

455. He (Dean) is, and Sam is his, and the demons are using it against them

456. A note saying 'help us'

457. Because he can see the demon's real face

458. True: Because he went to a neighbour for help

459. Lilith

460. Makes it holy by dropping rosary beads into a well

461. Ruby

462. She wakes up and Lilith isn't in the little girl anymore

463. Ruby

464. The hellhounds

465. In hell

Production, Crew and Writing

466. Jeremy Carver

467. Lou Bollo

468. Episode 3 'Bad Day at Black Rock', episode 9 'Malleus Maleficarum' and episode 14 'Long-Distance Call'

469. Sera Gamble

470. Serge Ladouceur

471. Two: Episode 1 'The Magnificent Seven' and episode 16 'No Rest for the Wicked'

472. Episode 12 'Jus in Bello'

473. Kim Manners

474. Episode 13 'Ghostfacers'

475. Robert Singer

Supernatural Trivia

476. Crushed by a falling piano, killed by a speeding car, chokes to death on a sausage, slips in the shower, food poisoning from tacos, electrocuted by an electric razor, fatally injured by Sam in a fight over an axe, killed by an arrow shot by the waitress at the diner, mauled to death by a dog

477. Episode 4 'Sin City' (by Casey)

478. Azazel

479. Nicholas Elia (episode 2 'The Kids are Alright')

480. Bustyasianbeauties.com

481. Norman Bates (from *Psycho*)

482. November (cover date Dec 2007/Jan 2008). The magazine ceased production at the end of 2012

483. Best Actor

484. *The Three Little Pigs, Hansel and Gretel, Cinderella, The Frog Prince, Little Red Riding Hood,* and *Snow White and the Seven Dwarfs*

485. *The Blair Witch Project*

486. Episode 12 'Jus in Bello'

487. The University of British Columbia

488. Sid Vicious (from punk band the Sex Pistols) and Nancy Spungen (Sid's girlfriend) who shared a drug-addicted lifestyle and died within a short time of one another (she was murdered and he died from a heroin overdose)

489. The Erie Motel

490. Episode 12 'Jus in Bello'

491. Rum, fruit syrup and grenadine

492. *The Magical Mystery Tour*

493. Dick Van Dyke

494. The Old Terminal Pub

495. *Groundhog Day*

496. *The X Files*

497. Stanley Kubrick (director of *The Shining*)

498. Lucy

499. Episode 1 'The Magnificent Seven'

500. Because of the Writers Guild of America strike

'Family don't end with blood.' ~ Bobby Singer

Also by
Light Bulb Quizzes
The Supernatural Quiz Book
Seasons 1 and 2

Coming soon
The Supernatural Quiz Book Season 4

Follow Light Bulb Quizzes on

Twitter: @LightBulbQuiz
and
Tumblr: lightbulbquizzes.tumblr.com

For news, giveaways
and forthcoming projects

Printed in Great Britain
by Amazon

50910715R00069